Awi-U-Sdi
Legend of Little Deer

Rachel, & Kristin

Awi-U-Sdi
Legend of Little Deer

Wado, Thank You

Wade Blevins

Wade Blevins

ozư

Illustrated by
Wade Blevins

Ozark Publishing, Inc.
P.O. Box 389
Redfield, Arkansas 72132

F
Ble   Blevins, Wade
      Legend of Little Deer, by Wade Blevins.
Illus. by Wade Blevins.
      Ozark Publishing, Inc., 1993.
      49P. illus. (Cherokee Indian Legend
Series)
      Summary: A small Indian boy learns the
secrets of hunting deer.
      1. Legends. I. Title. II. Series.

ISBN Casebound 1-56763-073-1
ISBN Paperback 1-56763-074-X

Ozark Publishing, Inc.
P.O. Box 389, 439 Rhoads Rd.
Redfield, AR 72132
Ph: 1-800-321-5671

Printed in the United States of America

ACKNOWLEDGMENT

I would like to thank my 103-year-old great-grandmother, who passed on her knowledge of the past to present and future generations and, in so doing, helped to preserve our Cherokee culture. Maude Parris Gardner, born of a Cherokee father and an English mother, was raised on the Illinois River in Indian Territory, now Oklahoma. Her stories of Cherokee superstitions and her knowledge of wild herbs and plants to be used as medicine and food have provided the family with hours of entertainment. In this age where everyone is attempting to find his or her identity, through her I know who I truly am. Through the efforts of

Native Americans, our culture will remain for our children and our children's children. It is not the color of one's skin, but the content of our heart that denotes a true A NI Y UN WI YA, a Cherokee. WA DO (Thank You).

FOREWORD

A small Indian boy learns of the Indian way to hunt deer.

Awi-U-Sdi
Legend of Little Deer

"Missed!" Dale shouted, watching the white flag of a ten-point buck disappear among the trees.

"That's okay, Dad; we've still got a few more days before deer season closes. He'll be back." Jesse methodically took the shells out of his gun, making sure it was empty before swinging it onto his shoulder.

"Yeah, but you're going to spend this weekend with your grandfather, remember? And I won't have any more free time before then."

"Maybe I can talk Mom into letting me visit the next weekend and stay here with you now," Jesse offered.

"I've already tried to talk your mother out of it, but she's not going to hear of it, son. She has got to be the most stubborn woman I've ever met. She says that this weekend is very important to her family and that you and she will go one way or the other, whether I like it or not."

Quietly, they made their way back through the Oklahoma timber and mist to the dirt road where their pickup was parked.

"I just don't understand it," said Jesse's father as he started the car. "It seems that every year the deer get harder and harder to find."

As they pulled into the drive-way of their four-bedroom house, Jesse's mother met each of them at the door with a kiss.

"Any luck?" she asked.

"Nah," grumbled Jesse's dad, "only got one shot off all day."

"Well, Tsan-U-Sdi, my youngest brother's son, got his first today. A nice twelve-point buck. Everyone is at Grandad's now, dressing it out."

"Aren't your other brothers out hunting today? Deer season closes in three days," commented Jesse's dad, sitting in his favorite chair and wrestling his boots off.

Jesse's mother looked a little uncomfortable. "No. They all killed their limit earlier this week."

"Hmph!" was all Jesse's father said as he made his way upstairs, shedding clothes as he went.

Jesse's mother just watched him stomp upstairs, sadly shaking her head. "Yonega," she said and laughed softly.

Jesse smiled because his mother often called his dad by her pet name "Yonega," or white man.

She meant it affectionately, although Jesse's dad was one-fourth Cherokee. Still, underneath the good-natured teasing, Jesse's mother felt that her husband should adopt more of the old ways.

"Go and get cleaned up, Jesse. We have a lot to do today. Grandfather will be expecting us for breakfast tomorrow."

The next morning, Jesse's mother was up before the sun had risen, shaking Jesse awake. "Hurry, we've got a two-hour drive ahead of us, and I want to get there to help with breakfast."

With a quick "Bye" to Dad and an extra feeding of Jesse's goldfish, they began the drive from Stillwell to the small Cherokee community of Kenwood, where Grandfather and most of the rest of his family lived.

Grandfather's house was a medium-sized cabin, constructed by him and his six brothers, Jesse was told by his mother. The house, as well as the smaller Asi, or traditional Cherokee sweatlodge located behind the house, faced the East toward the original homeland of the Cherokee people. The East was called "Nun-da-gun-ye," or Sunland. In the Sacred Medicine,

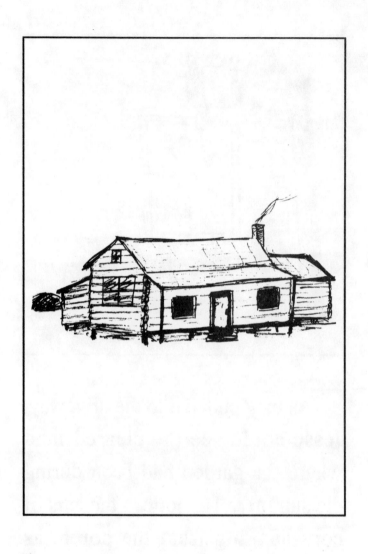

East is the direction connected with success and triump.

As they pulled into the driveway, Jesse could see the cleared land where the garden had been during the summer. He noticed the ears of corn hanging from the porch, as well as gourds of various shapes drying slowly in the frigid sunlight.

A couple of rangy hounds lazed in the sun, uninterested in the car that approached.

Grandfather was standing there on the porch waiting for them. He smiled warmly as they drew near, his long silver hair stirring with the early morning breeze.

"Si-yo, gi-yv-ha, we waited on breakfast for you," he said, standing aside so that Jesse and his mother could enter.

Inside, the house was alive with activity. Most of the men were in the front room talking and exchanging stories, while the women commandeered the kitchen, doing much more story swapping than cooking. The children were dispersed throughout the house, the number varying as groups of them slammed in and out the front and back doors.

Jesse's mom immediately went to the kitchen, tying a clean white apron on as she went, saying,

"Go talk to your grandfather and find out what you need to do. He said that maybe tomorrow you and he would go out hunting." With that, she sent him on his way, laughing at something one of her sisters had said, answering her in Cherokee spattered with English. Jesse, whose Cherokee went unused for the most part, only followed about half the conversation.

"What do you want me to do, Grandpa?" Jesse asked, standing beside him.

"After breakfast we'll help your uncles dress out the deer. Just stay by me, and I'll show you what to do."

Just then breakfast was served. Food and gossip were exchanged around the three tables set up for the family. Although the biggest part of the family lived nearby, when occasions such as these rolled around the whole family stayed at Grandfather's. It was always amazing how Grandfather's cabin could hold all of these people, but somehow everyone found a place.

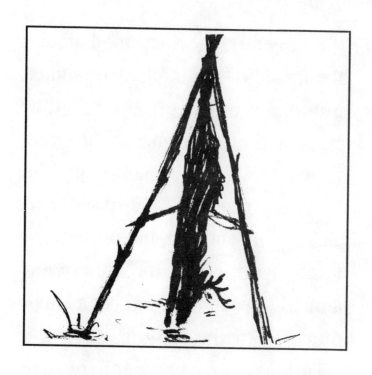

After the last of the dishes had been cleared away, everyone went outside where the ten deer had been hung to cool on game poles set up in a circle with an opening at the east end. In the center, a fire was burning brightly.

17

Silently, the men stood around the inside of the circle, the women along the outside. Grandfather stood in the very center of the circle facing east as he began to sing the song to Awi-U-Sdi, Little Deer, and to Ancient Red, the ceremonial fire. Finishing, he then went around to each deer and cut a small piece from the tongue, saying a small prayer over each before throwing them into the fire. Then he gave a prayer in Cherokee to the Christian God, whom all believed in, asking for prosperity in the coming year and thanking Him for the successful year already experienced.

Then they set about working, the men first carefully skinning the deer, the children carrying the heavy skins to the women, who stretched them out to remove the fat from the skin. Next the toes, or dewclaws, were removed to be made into leg rattles, and the head was split open for the brains, which were used in the long tanning process. Nothing was wasted; the insides were either eaten, used as sausage casing, or dried and used for traditional bow strings and lashings. Then the meat was cut; some was set aside to be smoked into sausage, jerky, and such, while the rest was to be frozen.

The air was full of laughing and teasing, and it looked more like a party than work. Jesse laughed and joked with his cousins, enjoying himself immensely. Everyone worked quickly and efficiently, skilled enough to laugh and talk while

slicing the slabs of meat almost
without thought. Soon nothing
was left. The meat was stored or
set in the smokehouse, the skins
were placed in large drums of
solution to loosen the hair, and the
other things were stored away to
be used later.

The women made their way to the kitchen to prepare dinner, while the young men ran races and set up a game of Cherokee marbles in the back yard. The older men sat on the porch, and the young children headed for the small creek, promising not to get wet. Jesse and some of his cousins were running footraces to the creek and back when his Aunt Egi came out the door calling everyone to the front room. Everyone straggled in, ready to eat. Several of the beans had split open during cooking, so Egi lined up all the babies, rubbing the cracked beans over their lips with a prayer to give them a smiling disposition. Everyone laughed when Egi's grandson immediately began to wail when the bean was passed over him.

Then they sat down to eat. Fresh deer, beans, hominy, cornbread, and watercress were served, with grape dumplings for dessert. Afterward, the dominoes and decks of cards

were brought out, the older ones preferring the traditional butterbean game.

The night passed quickly for Jesse, and much teasing, good-natured betting, and singing was passed around. As Jesse's Cherokee began to lose its rusty edges, he came to fully appreciate the special relationship found in his family, as well as the complexity of the language. He also came to appreciate more his mother's efforts to teach him to speak Cherokee. He now realized that she was not only trying to preserve a quickly disappearing tradition, but she also wanted Jesse to fully participate in her family's lives.

That night, sleeping arrangements were crowded as the children slept on the floor along with the younger adults. Everyone else crammed the five beds and couch. The oldest family members preferred to sleep in the warm Asi out back, claiming that it was better for their aching joints, but Mother told him that she thought it was to get away from the young ones' screaming and also to escape from the garrish English that spattered most of the family's conversations. Soon the whispers and giggling stilled and all was quiet.

Long before the sun had risen, Grandfather awakened Jesse. "Tse-sa-ni, it is time to go."

Silently, Jesse rose and followed Grandfather outside into the bitter morning chill. Together they walked through the silver morning, drinking the dew-laden air.

"Tell me, Tse-sa-ni," Grandfather began, using the Cherokee version of Jesse, "when you look out across this field, what do you see?"

Jesse shrugged, "Grass . . . dew . . . trees. Why?"

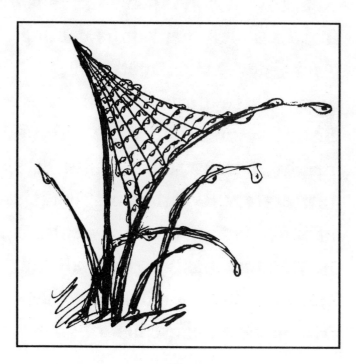

"To those who listen, the outdoors tells us much. For instance, the fact that there are still new cobwebs among the grasses tells us that we will have more warm weather to come. And look here. This snake died just this morning. See how it's lying on its back? This is a sign that rain is coming. And listen. Hear that? That's a Ji-gi-li-li twittering. There must be a fox or other large animal nearby, because the Ji-gi-li-li is a tattletale. By studying what's around us, a Cherokee realizes that Nature has given us all that we need. We should always thank her and never abuse her gifts."

They continued walking, Jesse now alert to the thousands of things going on around him. He felt as if the very earth were trying to speak to him.

They came to the creek, and Grandfather built a fire near the bank. He then began to undress and told Jesse to do the same. They both entered the water, dipping seven times while Grandfather recited prayers to Awi-U-Sdi, the chief of the Deer People. They then walked out to stand before the fire, Grandfather covering them both in smoke, followed by more prayer. Then Grandfather began telling Jesse about the deer.

"This is what my grandfathers told me when I was a boy. Awi-U-Sdi is the leader of all the deer. Whenever we hunt the deer, we sing to him to help us. The whole day, we don't eat out of respect for Awi-U-Sdi. After we kill a deer, we then ask forgiveness and thank the deer for its life. Otherwise, Awi-U-Sdi will ask the blood stains whether or not we said the proper prayers. If not, then Awi-U-Sdi will follow us and strike our limbs with "the crippler," or rheumatism, in the hunter. When a Cherokee is complaining about rheumatism, we always know that he has not performed the

proper songs to Awi-U-Sdi. It has always been so."

"Have you ever seen Awi-U-Sdi?" Jesse asked, eyes wide.

"Only once. When I was a young man, my mother and younger brothers were starving. The crops had withered on the vine, and no one here had enough to eat. I prayed and fasted for seven days. On the seventh day, a small deer of pure white appeared before me. Slowly, I raised my bow and shot seven white arrows into him. As he sank to the ground, I begged him to forgive me, but I needed his help because my family was going hungry. I carefully took a small piece from his antler and thanked him for his generous gift. He raised up, looked at me with understanding eyes, and ran

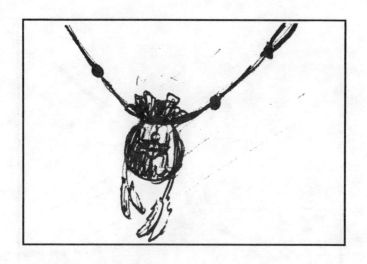

swiftly into the sky. I have worn
his gift ever since in this bag around
my neck." So saying, Jesse's
grandfather lifted the buckskin bag
reverently from his chest so Jesse
could see. It appeared almost to
glow softly against the coffee color
of Grandfather's hand. "Ever since
that time, I have always been able
to find the deer in the forest. This

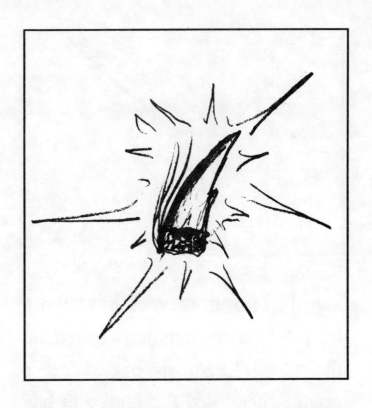

piece of antler is very powerful, and it is a great responsibility to use it wisely. We only take what our family can use and make sure that we use all of it. Come, Tse-sa-ni, we have a lot to do."

They walked deep into the woods for nearly an hour, with Grandfather pointing out the hundreds of different varieties of plant life and what the Cherokee used them for. "This is devils shoestring. The roots are used by the women to make their hair strong. Long ago, the stickball players would rub a salve of this on top of their skin to make their limbs tough. This is buckbrush. The Cherokee here in Oklahoma use it to make buckbrush baskets."

Grandfather talked quietly for the better part of an hour, seeming to know every plant in the forest and what it could be used for.

At last, they stopped in a clearing. "Now what?" asked Jesse.

"We sing," Grandfather replied. Softly he began to sing, calling the deer. After a few minutes, Jesse began singing . . .

O Deer you stand close by the tree
You sweeten your saliva with acorns,
Now you are standing near,
You have come where your
food rests on the ground.

All day they sang, and, as the sun began its final descent, Jesse heard a noise at the other end of the clearing. Softly, Grandfather began changing the song, asking the deer and his kin to forgive them. Jesse's heart quickened, and he felt himself a part of the chain of life, realizing the give-and-take that exists in everything around him. Then Jesse's gun leapt in his hands, and the shot echoed across the clearing.

As the deer fell, Jesse asked Grandfather, "What do we do now?"

"Now we thank the deer and pray over the blood drops."

Quickly, Grandfather cut out the back tendon, wrapping it with a bit of blood-soaked cloth. "The tendon is thrown away so that we will not become tired on long journeys, and the cloth of blood is offered to appease the water. It is believed that this deer will rise again from the blood stains we leave." With a final prayer asking Awi-U-Sdi not to afflict them with rheumatism, they took the buck home.

That night the family helped

dress the deer, putting the skin and meat with the others already dressed. Jesse was teased a lot by his uncles about how small it was and they bet that it was really Grandfather who shot it, but he knew that they were all proud of him.

Tse-sa-ni (Jesse) and his mother stayed all the next day helping tan the skins and distribute the meat to the oldest members of the family who couldn't travel. By the end of the day, all the meat and other goods had been divided equally, there being just enough for each household. Mother said that as soon as the skins were tanned, they would come back to collect their share and spend a few more days with the family. Jesse couldn't wait.

Toward evening, Jesse's father came. He said that he'd had no luck all weekend, but he was extremely proud of Jesse for his accomplishment.

As they were leaving, Jesse noticed that his dad was limping. "Rheumatism bothering you again, Dad?" he asked.

"Yeah, I don't understand it, but every year around deer season it starts acting up."

Jesse smiled a secret smile and began to hum a song to Awi-U-Sdi, chief of the Deer People.

GLOSSARY

YO-NE-GAS	WHITE MAN
NUN-DA-GUN-YE	THE EAST
SI-YO	HELLO
GI-YV-HA	COME IN
AWI-U-SDI	LITTLE DEER
TSE-SA-NI	JESSE
JI-GI-LI-LI	CHICKADEE
ASI	SWEATLODGE

FOOD

Every July my great-grandmother
would roam the woods in search of
summer grapes. Although the
grapes didn't ripen until later, she
would pick the green grapes to
make her specialty, green grape
jelly. When she gathered them, she
would be sure to gather too many
and use the plumpest to put into
dumplings.

After washing them thoroughly, she
put them into a large pot with

plenty of fresh water and enough sugar to sweeten the grapes. She then boiled them until tender. To this boiling mixture she added drop dumplings, covered and cooked until the dumplings were done.

REMEDY

Although most Cherokee people were rarely bothered by poison ivy, if by chance they caught it, they would rub the flesh of the ji-s-dv-na, or crawfish, on it to help it heal.

The crawfish, which is now almost a staple food in many Cherokee homes, was not eaten. Traditionally, it was believed that the meat was rotten due to its red color.

SUPERSTITION

The Cherokee people have always had a great fear of witches. The most common way to protect against a witch's spell was to hang a buzzard feather above the door.